Nana's Orchard

written by
Carol Gould

illustrated by
Paul Drzewiecki

KAEDEN ❤ BOOKS™

In Nana's orchard there are rows and rows of trees.

Bobby runs up and down
the rows of trees
in Nana's orchard.

Bobby climbs the trees
in Nana's orchard.

"Don't fall!" yells Bobby's dad.

Bobby runs from tree to tree picking apples in Nana's orchard.

"Be careful! Don't drop the apples!" shouts the apple picker.

Bobby rides on the tractor up and down the rows of trees in Nana's orchard.

Bobby skis up and down
the rows of trees in
Nana's orchard. Winter in
Nana's orchard is Bobby's
favorite time of year.